MONSIEUR

Originally published in French as *Monsieur* by Editions de
Minuit, 1986
First published in the United States and Great Britain in 1991
by Marion Boyars Publishers

First Dalkey Archive Edition, 2008
Published by arrangement with Marion Boyars Publishers

Library of Congress Cataloging-in-Publication Data

Toussaint, Jean-Philippe.
 [Monsieur. English]
 Monsieur / Jean-Philippe Toussaint ; translation by John
Lambert.
    p. cm.
 ISBN-13: 978-1-56478-505-3 (alk. paper)
 ISBN-10: 1-56478-505-X (alk. paper)
 I. Lambert, John, 1960- II. Title.
 PQ2680.O86M6613 2008
 843'.914--dc22
                                    2007045789

Partially funded by a grant from the Illinois Arts Council, a state
agency, and by the University of Illinois at Urbana-Champaign

www.dalkeyarchive.com

Printed on permanent/durable acid-free paper
and bound in the United States of America

MONSIEUR

jean-philippe toussaint

translated from the French by John Lambert

Dalkey Archive Press
Champaign and London

The day, three years ago, when Monsieur took up his new assignment, he was given his own office on the sixteenth floor of the Leonardo da Vinci Tower. So far so good. The room was spacious, with a fairly high ceiling. A large tinted bay window looked out over the city. The desk, within arms' reach of two identical metal shelves, had six drawers on either side, and was topped with a thick plate of smoked glass. The chair swivelled, Monsieur casually assured himself.

The following days, Monsieur spent the best part of his mornings putting the office in order. He emptied the cupboards, one after the other, dumped the contents of the drawers onto the carpet. Then, working methodically through the mess, he filled plastic bags with old newspapers and whole stacks of magazines, which he started to store in the hall, behind his door. He put his predecessor's books into boxes and replaced them on the shelves with his own files.

Little by little, he settled in. The next day he brought in an electric coffee-maker, which he plugged into the sole outlet in the room tucked away behind the coat rack, and which, for the time being, he left on a crate of old books. His coffee-maker made excellent coffee, and kept it nice and warm. Each morning he drank a cup or two, never failing to offer some to his guests.

Very quickly, Monsieur became rather well liked within the firm. Although remaining distant with his colleagues, he didn't neglect, on occasion, to join in some hallway conversation where, eyes lowered, he listened to this or that question being discussed. Then, taking leave, he turned and made his way nonchalantly back to his office, running one hand along the corridor walls.

In the course of the morning it was not unusual for Monsieur to go down to the ground floor and spend a few moments in the large glass-enclosed hall. Coming round the information desk, he would head for the cafeteria, where he bought a packet of chips, paprika chips, for example, why not, which he opened while resuming his leisurely walk. He would linger before the union noticeboard and, well enough acquainted with the history of the labour movement, he read the notices thoughtfully, eating a chip from time to time. Then, turning round, he would go back across the hall, picking up a few brochures intended for the general public on the way. He would quickly browse through some and leave others on a bench, waiting for the elevator.

Twice a week, a pile of newspapers and specialized economic and financial journals awaited

Monsieur at the bottom of his in-tray. He took them into his office and read them over, leafing through them all, annotating certain articles with the fine point of his *Rotring,* cutting out others, which he kept in plastic folders.

Indeed, in the middle of the afternoon Monsieur would go back down to the cafeteria. He hitched up his trousers, sat down comfortably and ordered a small beer. These were calm hours, the lobby was often deserted. From his table he could see the large aquarium, where tranquil creatures went hither and thither in the clear water. There weren't a lot of people in the cafeteria at that time. A couple of receptionists from the information desk would eat cassatas and talk over coffee at a neighbouring table.

When, returning to his office, Monsieur found himself in the elevator with the Chief Executive, he would ask him which floor he wanted and push the appropriate button. On the way up they would look at the walls of the elevator, each at a different spot. Monsieur kept his eyes lowered. The Chief Executive, for his part, played with his key ring. Sometimes they exchanged a few select words. The Chief Executive listened attentively to Monsieur, arms crossed, all the while seeming to ask himself who on earth he could possibly be.

Each Thursday, Monsieur attended a meeting with the Chief Executive that brought together a large number of company executives. A notice tacked up in the main hall of his floor gave the time of the meeting, which was always in the same place, a large rectangular office in which an oval lacquered table took up all the space. A blotting pad and an ash-tray were set before each chair. Monsieur sat at the seventeenth seat on the left where, he knew from experience, his presence went the most unnoticed, beside Madame Dubois-Lacour who, as supervisor to a large part of his activities, responded to most of the questions asked of him and, throughout the meeting, calmly smoked his cigarette. Monsieur was scrupulously attentive to remain in line with her body, drawing back when she moved backwards, leaning forward when she moved forward, so as to be never too directly exposed. Whenever the Chief Executive said his name out loud, Monsieur leaned forward, as if surprised and, inclining his head respectfully, responded straight away in dry, precise, technical, professional terms. Hip, hop. After which, fingers trembling slightly, he retreated into his neighbour's shadow. The meetings, in general, lasted a little less than an hour. When the Chief Executive finally adjourned, everyone got up in turn and put on their coats; small groups formed (you haven't seen my Havanitos, said Madame Dubois-Lacour, a red and gold pack).

Dubois-Lacour sometimes brought files to his office. Monsieur asked her to sit down; she handed him the documents and, crossing her legs, thank you, summarized some of them, drew his attention to others, going over their major points. Then, adding a final clarification, she left him alone. Dubois-Lacour never, and for this he was grateful, doubted the seriousness with which Monsieur approached his work. You always seem to be bone idle, she said to him amiably on occasion, adding, not without finesse, that this was the sign of the truly great worker.

When Monsieur was expecting visitors in his office, a secretary would telephone him to inform him of their arrival. He waited at his desk, or better still, stood pensively before the large bay window, fixing his tie. They came in, Monsieur offered them coffee. Slowly turning his spoon in his cup; he asked them to be seated and heard them out while looking at his fingers, trying at all times to remain friendly. To the most persistent, those who didn't hesitate to make him sweat slightly, who insisted adamantly this time on obtaining precise facts, figures, something more concrete, he promised charts and even graphics. And, once they'd left, he seriously considered their requests.

People, really.

One evening a week, Monsieur played indoor football on the cheap in a local gym. He kept apart from the team in the locker room. He took his time getting changed. He had a very smart outfit, red T-shirt, cotton bermudas and double-soled tennis shoes. He arrived the last on the pitch and started warming up with the others, under the eyes of ten or so girls in track suits who looked on and commented from the sidelines. During the match, each time there was a corner kick, Monsieur, who played defense, came forward and, placing himself in front of the opposing goal, got ready to head the ball into the net. All right, big fellow, back you go, said the coach, a former ace. Monsieur, shrugging his shoulders, trotted back to his place, keeping one eye on the pitch.

Monsieur was not at all fond of anything that reminded him of himself. No. The night he sprained his wrist, for example, he was reading the newspaper while waiting for the bus, his duffle bag at his feet. A man beside him attempted to ask him something. As Monsieur didn't answer, finishing his article, the man, smiling carefully, thought it appropriate to repeat his question. Monsieur lowered his paper and looked him up and down absently, top to bottom. The man got nearer and gave him an abrupt shove. Losing his balance, Monsieur stumbled into the metal edge of the bus shelter with his full weight.

At the time Monsieur was engaged.

Yes. It must have been rather distressing for his fiancée to see him arrive that evening, slightly hurt. She got some ice cubes from the kitchen and, stroking his head to soothe him, told him to put his hand in the ice bucket. Then, while Monsieur took off his watch, she sat cross-legged on the carpet and, in an attempt to relax the atmosphere he did nothing to lighten, going from the description he had given her of the man's appearance, sketched a quick portrait, which she tacked up on the wall in the entrance hall.

That night, Monsieur's fiancée showed herself capable of a great deal of understanding, putting up a makeshift cot in her room, supporting him when he had to give, with all possible delicacy, an explanation to her parents. The latter, the Parrains, whom Monsieur had found rather easy-going when he first met them, were now standing in the doorway, leaning towards him. Sitting on the bed, Monsieur, who didn't want a fuss, tried to justify his presence in their apartment, speaking slowly, persuasively, in an attempt to get them on his side. But they hardly listened. What they wanted to know, because it intrigued them, was why their daughter had put up a picture of their friend Caradec in the hall.

The next day, in the early hours of the morning, coming soundlessly across the hall, Monsieur bumped into his fiancée's mother, dressed in a nightie and sleepy-eyed, who seemed almost surprised to find herself at home. Monsieur, to help her orientate herself, briefly reminded her of his name and greeted her politely with his eyes lowered, looking at her stomach, at the bottom of which there appeared through the thin material a fine early morning display of pubic hair. Did you sleep well? she asked him, right hand on her left shoulder, co-ordinating her movements so as to be seen in profile. Monsieur shook his head and showed his wrist which had ballooned alarmingly during the night. She looked at it from a distance and, speaking vaguely of hospitals and X-rays, added while shuffling off sideways that he should be careful with the flush in the bathroom (right, said Monsieur).

After wandering round the apartment, the layout of which gave him some trouble, Monsieur entered the kitchen, clean and tidy, dressed in a midnight-blue suit and a dark tie. He pulled on the creases of his trousers and sat down. Monsieur Parrain was sitting at the table in his undershirt and observed Monsieur out of the corner of his eye while smoking a cigarette. Monsieur's fiancée was still asleep according to the latest news. That shouldn't stop them, her mother and he decided, from starting breakfast without her. Eager to make a good impression, Monsieur did not hesitate, despite the state of his wrist, to get up and pour himself more coffee.

Madame Parrain was still wearing her nightie, but she had put on a loose pair of panties underneath, so that Monsieur could now only see her breasts, with which he contented himself as he drank his coffee. Monsieur Parrain, meanwhile, stubbing his cigarette in a saucer, asked Monsieur if he could examine his wrist, just curious. He took his glasses from their case, took the time to adjust them and asked Monsieur to be good enough to crouch down in front of him right on the tiles in such a way that his arm would rest freely on his thigh. When Monsieur was installed, Monsieur Parrain kneaded his wrist for a few moments without conviction, before saying in a solicitous tone, taking off his glasses, that he'd have to get an X-ray as you couldn't see a thing.

Monsieur knew full well that X-rays were common, painless procedures, and he would have gone along without too much apprehension if, to go through with it, he didn't have to go to the hospital (Monsieur was not particularly fond of hospitals). And so, sitting down again, he asked the Parrains if by any chance there wasn't a doctor in the building, for example a radiologist. Aside from Doctor Douvres on the third floor, they replied that no, there were none. Monsieur asked what they had against Doctor Douvres, but Madame Parrain protested, nothing at all, that he was a neighbour, just a neighbour, she said, I assure you there's never been anything between us.

While Madame Parrain washed the dishes without further ado, not knowing what to do in the kitchen (he had already helped by clearing away his cup), Monsieur searched his pockets and took out assorted slips of paper, which he started to burn thoughtfully over the ashtray, asking Madame Parrain if Doctor Douvres made house calls. Madame Parrain seemed a bit put out, he thought, not to be able to answer. He had only to ring him up, she said, to find out.

Monsieur was not particularly fond of the telephone.

Monsieur placed his hands flat on the table, lifted a finger to look at his nail, then, having considered it critically, gave a small slap on the table and left the room. In the hall, he asked Monsieur Parrains' permission to use the telephone. He was heading for the bathroom, carrying a toolbox. When, after his call, Monsieur reappeared in the kitchen, his fiancée was there, smoking a cigarette with her cup of tea. You know doctor Douvres' number? asked Madame Parrain. No, no, said Monsieur matter-of-factly, no more than you, and explained that he had rung his boss, so he wouldn't worry. Oh, I didn't know you worked, said Madame Parrain. And what do you do? she said. He's a commercial director, said his fiancée. Indeed, said Monsieur, sitting down. Yes, yes, said his fiancée, he's one of the three or four most important commercial directors for Fiat France.

Indeed, said Monsieur.

And do you get good rates? asked Madame Parrain. Sorry? said Monsieur. Do you get good rates on the cars? I don't know, said Monsieur, tapping on the table. You should find out, she said. Yes, if you like, said Monsieur, I'll find out. Fine, fine. Any other questions?

After waiting several minutes in the company of Doctor Douvres' assistant, Monsieur, who had finally made up his mind to consult him, was shown into his office, a large room with beige walls, a large desk and a medical couch covered with a white sheet. Very tall and elegant in his white coat, Doctor Douvres was a man of around fifty, thin and distinguished looking who, getting up to welcome Monsieur, shook his hand and, rather than sit down again, started to talk to him about one thing and another, advancing towards him while Monsieur retreated. Finally backing Monsieur into a corner without letting up on his persistent patter, he sized him up discreetly to see if he was, or wasn't, taller than him (people, really). Then he went and sat down. Putting his hands flat on the desk, he asked what was wrong. Monsieur explained. As he explained more and more Doctor Douvres became more and more understanding and told him he'd have a look right away, if Monsieur would take off his jacket. All the while examining his wrist very delicately, he asked a number of questions, to which he responded himself, no less, sometimes succinctly, other times in far more detail, telling Monsieur that he would have to press on the bone, which might hurt and, in the same courteously offhand tone, asked what he did in life. In life? said Monsieur. Not put off in the slightest by his feint, Doctor Douvres, lifting his head good-naturedly, repeated his question, which he formed nonetheless a bit differently to force an answer. Monsieur anwered evasively. And it's interesting? asked Doctor Douvres. Yes, I'm paid well, said Monsieur. I think I earn more money than you do, he added. After that, Doctor Douvres kept quiet (this was perhaps how Monsieur should have started).

When he got back to the Parrains' apartment, Monsieur rang his office. Speaking politely to the secretary, he asked her please to cancel all his appointments and let Madame Dubois-Lacour know that he would be absent until the beginning of the next week. Then, going into his fiancée's room to collect his things, he came back to the kitchen with his duffle bag and his brief case. As her husband was sitting down, Madame Parrain told him that their daughter's fiancé was a commercial manager. Commercial director, said Monsieur. Yes. I do a bit of public relations as well, but it's not my strong point.

No. Monsieur, delicately massaging his wrist, told his fiancée he was thinking of making the best of these few days off work by going to Cannes. As his fiancée, surprised, wanted to know what he was going to do in Cannes, Monsieur said he didn't know, he'd see when he got there. Any other questions? No. Fine. The journey went well. On the train, Monsieur found himself in a compartment with a German-speaking Swiss man.

At Cannes Monsieur checked into the first hotel he came across, not far from the station.

In the morning, he ate breakfast in a café in the centre. He bought the papers and bet on horses, racking up modest winnings, occasionally thinking of going some time in person to the nearby track at Cagnes-sur-Mer, to get the thrill of being in the stands. And so time passed. In the afternoon, for example, around tea time, he played billiards in the smoky back room of a café with a small, taciturn old man who sometimes stopped during the game for a bowl of Cannestrellis. The old chap had been pretty good at billiards in his youth, but he was no match for Monsieur. No. Nevertheless, they played together, became friends. One evening, a kind gesture, the old codger invited him to dinner.

Two days before leaving, Monsieur rang up a friend, Louis, who had a house in the hills above Vence. He invited him, this friend, to come and stay for a few days and, that afternoon, came to Cannes and picked him up in his Volkswagen.

In the car, climbing towards Vence on the wet roads, Monsieur, disconsolately rummaging in the glove compartment in search of a cigar, told Louis about Schrödinger's experiment in subsumed probability, where a cat was placed in a closed chamber with a capsule of cyanide and a potentially radioactive atom in a detection device in such a way that, if the atom underwent a radioactive deterioration, the detector would activate a mechanism that would break open the capsule and kill the cat. (People, really). But that wasn't all. The atom in question having in fact a fifty percent probability of undergoing this radioactive deterioration within the hour, the question was the following: sixty minutes later, was the cat alive or dead? It had to be one or the other, no? Try to keep your eyes on the road, said Monsieur. However, according to the Copenhagen interpretation, he went on, when the hour was up the cat was in limbo, with a fifty percent chance of being alive, and an equal chance of being dead. One could always take a quick peek to find out, you will say, a quick peek hardly posing a risk of killing it, nor of bringing it back to life if it was dead. But, still according to the Copenhagen interpretation, the simple fact of taking a look would radically alter the mathematical description of its state, transforming it from the state of limbo to a new state, where it was either positively alive or positively dead, as may be.

Everything is as may be.

Oh yes. After dinner, late in the evening, they walked under an umbrella to sober up, Monsieur and Louis, in the soaked gardens around the house. Their elegant shoes caked with mud, they found their way in the dark with an electric torch, preceded by Louis' dog, probably a spaniel, Monsieur thought, which, stopping occasionally to wait for them, shook itself in the beam of the flash light.

Early the next morning while Louis was still asleep, Monsieur walked for some time in his bare feet on the wet grass, ate breakfast alone peering into the distance. A hammock in the garden, object of every desire, hung between a plane tree and a dead mimosa. Imperceptibly, Monsieur let himself sink into the hammock, lulled by the soft breeze, legs crossed, eyes open, his thoughts following the rhythm of the hammock's swinging movements, not anticipating nor provoking them. Occasionally, putting one hand behind him on the smooth trunk of the plane tree, he pushed for an instant to stop the movement; then, giving a shove, he started the hammock swinging again, from left to right, for hours at a time.

In the late afternoon, he and Louis went to cut wood in a small clearing below the house. They sawed for an hour or two, then went in, leaving the bigger logs, which were too heavy to carry, where they lay. The smaller branches, and even the larger branches, they heaved onto their shoulders and pulled along behind them. The long and shady trail rose slowly back toward the house.

Then came the time for Monsieur to go back to Paris.

In the evening, sometimes, after dinner, Monsieur played scrabble in the kitchen with his fiancée's parents; he kept score himself on a sheet of paper divided into three columns. Disputes over the spelling of this or that word never went very far as Monsieur, in the event of a difference of opinion, allowed them to appeal to the dictionary, and if, in doing so, they discreetly branched out into the surrounding pages and started to cheat, Monsieur didn't let on. Bit by bit, the Parrains adopted Monsieur, finding him easy to get on with, always ready to be of help.

Monsieur, like Paul Guth, was the very picture of the ideal son-in-law.

Since they had split up, however, his fiancée and he, it was possible that the Parrains had a few qualms about having him stay on. Monsieur, to tell the truth, would have been hard put to say why his fiancée and he had separated. He had followed the whole thing rather from a distance, in fact, remembering only that the number of things he had been reproached for had seemed to him considerable.

Monsieur's fiancée, since she had been seeing a certain Jean-Marc, an elderly married businessman, now took to staying out more and more often and, when she did come home for dinner, she remained very cold with Monsieur, almost aloof. As for the Jean-Marc in question, it was only on special occasions that he spoke to him at all. With the Parrains, however, he hadn't even removed his overcoat before he started fawning all over them, hoping perhaps that they would turn a blind eye to his liaison with their daughter (who was still a minor, after all).

As for Monsieur, he continued to maintain the best relations with everyone. The Parrains, for example, who, without seeking to understand his reasons, had got the message that Monsieur had no particular desire to go back to live with his brother, made every effort to encourage him to find a new place. In the morning, when he came in after his shower to have breakfast with them dressed in his bathrobe, they never failed to inquire into the progress of his search, and it was Madame Parrain even, who, really very nicely, took things in hand one day, and finally found him a three-room apartment in the neighbourhood.

Monsieur's new apartment, which had three large rooms, was practically empty and smelled of paint. Only in his bedroom were there one or two pieces of furniture and a few camping chairs. All the other rooms were empty, with the exception of the entrance, where he had put his suitcases, as well as two boxes of magazines and a portable typewriter. Since the previous day Monsieur hadn't touched or unpacked a thing. He sat in the bedroom, the light out, in a reclining chair. Dressed in a grey suit, a white shirt and a dark tie that everyone envied him, he listened to the radio and touched himself all over his body, his cheeks, or his sex, coolly, at random, but no comfort, really, came to him from having himself permanently at hand.

And, that evening in his new apartment, Monsieur remained quite simply in this position for hours, where the absence of pain was a pleasure, and the absence of pleasure a pain, bearable in its presence. His reclining chair, of navy-blue cloth, allowed three positions, which Monsieur adopted in turn, following the hours of the night, from the most upright to the most inclined. Well into the evening he lowered the supporting brackets of the seat to the lowest notches and let himself slide back, his eyes closed, an inch or so from the ground.

Near eleven o'clock, out of the blue, someone rang at the door. Yes. Slowly opening his eyes, he could hardly believe it. Monsieur let his gaze travel back and forth across the ceiling for a few moments and, finally getting up as best he could, crossed the hall to open the door. It was a man he didn't know who, standing sideways in the dim light of the stairwell, told him that they were neighbours, which seemed to delight the fellow. (People, really). My name's Kaltz, he said, Kaltz, and he held out his hand. Assuring him that he did not intend to stay long, he side-stepped Monsieur to take a look at the apartment, wanting to know on the way what Monsieur did in life. He, Kaltz, was a geologist, mineralogist, if Monsieur preferred. He was a research assistant at the CNRS. He had just come back from a week's holiday in Corfu, he said, he was forty-seven years old. That's possible, said Monsieur, and he asked him to stay for a drink, a glass of wine for example, it was all he had.

Sitting across from him on the bed, Kaltz explained to Monsieur that, as they were now neighbours, they would be able to do many things together and, without wasting a breath, smoothing the bedspread with the palm of his hand, had told him of his project to write a treatise on mineralogy, the general thesis of which he started to outline for Monsieur. Very quickly, moreover, becoming more and more enthusiastic as he elaborated on his methodology, he began trying to convince him that they should work together; he had all the elements of the book in his head, he said, knew a photographer and a cartographer, all he had left to do was write the text, for the editing of which he would be happy to engage his services. If you agree, he added. Monsieur looked at him. As the silence began to make itself felt, and as he seemed to be waiting for a response, Monsieur asked out of curiosity how long he thought it would take. A year, he said. Monsieur helped himself to more wine, deliberately, and, in a friendly tone, setting the bottle on the floor, admitted that he didn't have a huge amount of time at the moment, adding that in any event he knew nothing about mineralogy, to say the least. Not to worry, said Kaltz, and explained that he'd take care of everything, Monsieur would have nothing to do, just simply to copy the text under his dictation. I'll have a little more wine, please, he said. Then, to tempt Monsieur all the more, he hinted that they could share the rights, two thirds one third, assuring him that the work would be published, probably in Stuttgart he thought, by a scientific publisher whose prestigious name he dropped modestly. As, again, he seemed to be waiting for an answer, Monsieur finally asked him if, as he planned to have the book published in Stuttgart, it was Stuttgart was it not, it would not be more judicious to think of writing it in German. Kaltz didn't balk and said they could very easily have it translated into German, their book, or even have it published in France. So, we're agreed? he asked.

Monsieur didn't know how to say no.

The world of minerals, and of crystals in particular, fascinates not only certain specialists, but also, increasingly, the general public. All rocks, even the softest, are in reality made up of crystals, rarely visible to the naked eye, and it is not by chance that, until the beginning of the twentieth century, almost nothing was known of their composition. It was only with the discovery of X-rays, and with the experiments of von Laue, who conceived of bombarding crystals to photograph the emergent rays, that a new branch of science was born: crystallography.

Every weekend now (Monsieur worked weekdays) Kaltz dictated his work. Pacing his room carrying a folder of diverse documents, his glasses up on his forehead, thinking hard, his various papers spread out on the quilt, he progressed in his work at a steady pace. Sitting at his desk, Monsieur typed the text on the typewriter, lifting his head from time to time to ask him more precisely what he meant. The first days, lost in his notes and very agitated, Kaltz got irritated at being interrupted, a little too often he said, by Monsieur's questions, and even allowed himself to comment ironically on the fact that he typed with just two fingers, but as Monsieur had quickly put him in his place, and rather sharply, he made an effort now to dictate more slowly.

Beryl, mit ein y, ore compound of aluminium and beryllium, is a hexagonal crystal, while topaz, as we have shown above, is an orthorhombic aluminum fluorosilicate. Garnets, similarly, silicate compounds of aluminium and calcium, magnesium, iron, manganese or chrome, are used in jewellery for their cubic forms.

Monsieur finally reported all this to Madame Dubois-Lacour.

Dubois-Lacour, on the telephone (Monsieur was calling from a pay phone; his neighbour was upstairs in his room), described the course of events, started by saying that he should have made a point of refusing the proposition straight away, adding that now the best thing to do was to try, very simply, to get him to understand that he couldn't give up all his weekends. Then, becoming somewhat irritated with Monsieur, who fatalistically stuck to repeating that in his opinion it had become insoluble, she concluded, at her wits' end, that he could get along quite well on his own, no?

No. The situation was hopeless.

Native gold, very rare, known and coveted since the earliest of times, magnificent in its hues, belongs in its crystalline state to the cubic system. Considered traditionally as the most precious of the metals, gold is the perfect mineral, of inexhaustible symbolism: symbol of knowledge for the Brahmans, for the Aztecs, the earth's new skin. A more spiritual significance is to be observed with the Dogon people, for whom gold is the quintessence of copper, and the symbol of purifying fire and illumination, as indicated by the word sanuya, which could be translated as Reinheit, meaning purity, derived from sanu, meaning gold: ZAHAV.

It struck Monsieur that the best solution was to move out.

Dubois-Lacour proposed to accompany him on a visit to the new apartment that she'd found him, a room in fact, with a family. At six o'clock, leaving the office together, they went down to the basement parking lot where her little car was jammed between two concrete columns. Explaining to Monsieur that she had good prospects of being part of the delegation the company was sending to Japan, she put her two little dogs in the back and, getting in, leaned over to open the door for Monsieur. Monsieur gathered the folds of his coat around him and, bending over, one leg first, managed to scrunch up and join her. She hit the pedal and they burst outside just as Monsieur was doing up his seat belt.

Quite a bit later, they drove down a narrow street in a far-flung neighbourhood. Dubois-Lacour slowed down and stopped in front of an old building bordered with a small fenced garden. She gave him the necessary directions and dropped him there, unable to accompany him any further as she had become late in all the traffic. Standing on the pavement Monsieur watched Simone's car speed off. When it was gone, he took a few steps in the street. It was silent, deserted. He kept walking a while in the neighbourhood, went into a café, where he drank a beer, bought some cigarettes. Then, coming back the same way, he appeared again in front of the building.

What to do?

The front, clean and dull, had just been re-painted. The windows on the second floor, his destination, were closed, two of them with metal shutters. In the dark front hall, looking for the light switch, Monsieur stopped before the mail-boxes and absently read over the names of the tenants. Then, somewhat undecidedly, he started off up the stairs. The steps were large, covered by a carpet held down with thin brass rods. Arriving at the first floor landing, he hesitated and, giving himself a last reprieve, went back downstairs and took the elevator.

The second-floor apartment had a huge dou-ble door of darkish wood, each half ornamented with a silver knocker. Monsieur knocked very gently and, hearing no noise, got ready to leave when the other door on the landing opened be-hind him. He spun round, explaining that he was looking for Monsieur or Madame Leguen. The man who had opened the door said that he was Monsieur Leguen and, showing Monsieur into a large dark entrance hall, looked him up and down for a moment in silence before asking him to be good enough to come this way. They went down several corridors, crossed a large dining room where an elderly woman was having dinner, good evening Madame, and proceeded to the other end of the apartment, right into his office. There, sitting down at a small desk, Monsieur Leguen asked him a certain number of questions, wanted to know his age—twenty-nine.

After a brief panoramic view of their common friends, limited, in fact, to Madame Dubois-Lacour (Simone, he had known her for ever) Monsieur Leguen explained to Monsieur that, if he had chosen to rent this room to a student, it was not, of course, for the twelve hundred odd francs he was asking. You are still a student, I believe? But, before he could answer, he assured Monsieur immediately that he wasn't particularly intent on having a student. No, they had simply thought, his wife and he, that their lodger could perhaps, once or twice a week, give their son some instruction in his school work. Ludovic, you see, he said playing thoughtfully with his paper knife, has very eclectic tastes for a boy of fifteen. He's a film buff, a Hellenist. But in class, how shall I say it, he's a bit rebellious when it comes to adapting to a too rigid, often constraining routine. He's failed a year, he said, and stood up to show him the room.

There reigned, in Monsieur's room, an odor of wax mixed with dried semen. The curtains were pulled. The dark wooden floors seemed even more sombre in the dull light. It's my mother's room, said Monsieur Leguen in a hushed voice. Yes, I see, whispered Monsieur. Against one wall there was an ancient mirrored table, fitted with a washbasin. A crucifix hung over the bed, and a few faded photos in carved frames stood here and there. Monsieur Leguen, after lighting the bedside lamp, opened the cupboard to show Monsieur the shelves, very clean, with wallpaper tacked up inside. They considered the shelves for a moment, approvingly, then, each closing one door of the cupboard, left the room. There, said

Monsieur Leguen, if you want you can move in as soon as the end of the week.

No.

Monsieur had said no. Monsieur Leguen considered him a moment, objectively, and, assuring him that he understood, added that in any event he could still think it over. Then, very courteously, he closed the door and showed him out. Walking slowly one behind the other, they went back along the hall and, making their way through the apartment, crossed the dining room, where the old woman who was eating dinner watched them go back the other way, giving them a tender look.

Thus, crystals found in nature are not always perfect and may show certain defects, such as dislocations or piling faults, which the diffraction of X-rays will bring out, either locally through topographies, or globally through the reflected intensity of the whole crystal. Someone rang at the door. Surprised, Kaltz interrupted his dictation, his notes in his hand, and turned to Monsieur, a little miffed, giving him a questioning look to see if he was expecting someone. No, no. I'll investigate, he said and, before Monsieur could move, he left the room, turning round to tell him on the way out that it was no doubt Madame Pons-Romanov (whom, he added, he had taken the liberty of asking to come by that evening).

Ushered by Kaltz into the apartment, a somewhat ill-at-ease Madame Pons-Romanov, if it was she, was standing in Monsieur's room, a blonde, apparently timid woman, who wore a light-coloured fur coat that suited her quite well. Kaltz invited her to take a seat on the reclining chair. She sat down gingerly and put her handbag on her knees, giving Monsieur an embarrassed smile from time to time. Kaltz, who paid her no further attention, straightened some papers on the bed, reread his notes. I'll be with you in a minute, he said, I just want to finish up here. He opened several folders, and, explaining that he couldn't find a document he needed, left the room to look for it in his flat, leaving Monsieur alone with Madame Pons-Romanov.

Monsieur, who had no idea who this woman could be, remained seated at his desk for a few moments and couldn't keep himself from sneaking a glance at her now and then. Then, as Kaltz was taking his time getting back, he got up and sat down on his bed beside Madame Pons-Romanov, who, sitting very straight in the reclining chair, occasionally slipped a foot from her shoe to rub it delicately against her leg while looking shyly at Monsieur. Monsieur who, each time their eyes met, continued to respond politely to her smiles, finally resolved to engage her in conversation, asking if she was a friend of Kaltz's. She said no, not really, she hardly knew him.

Fine. Monsieur, after a moment, got up and, waiting for Kaltz to get back, went absently over his typescript. Finding a couple of mistakes on one page, he opened his bottle of correcting fluid and touched it up here and there with surgical strokes before blowing softly on the page. Then, as Kaltz still had not returned, he lit a cigarette and, approaching Madame Pons-Romanov's reclining chair, always the good host, held out the packet and offered her one.

When he reappeared in the apartment, Kaltz excused himself for having made them wait and, taking it for granted that Madame Pons-Romanov knew what Monsieur and he were expecting of her, invited any further questions she might have, including those regarding payment, for example. Then, giving it another thought, he added that, for the whole book, there shouldn't be more than twenty or so maps, the only ones presenting any difficulties, in his view, being the stratigraphies because, as he had already mentioned to her on an earlier occasion, rather than proceeding by traditional sections, he still wondered if it wouldn't be possible, from a classic chorochromatic map, to superimpose colours onto each of the separately enclosed areas. Madame Pons-Romanov had no objections and, turning to Monsieur, said that, yes, in her view they could always try.

Monsieur, who saw no great difficulties one way or the other, stood with his back to the window and was beginning to see that if Kaltz had taken his time coming back, it was not that he had looked in vain for this or that document but simply that he had gone and changed. Having shed his usual limp jacket and scarf, he was now wearing an elegant grey alpaca suit, a white shirt and a bow-tie. Thus attired, he had perched on the edge of the bed and, legs crossed, was holding Madame Pons-Romanov in conversation over the last article that she had published in a journal co-edited by the CNRS, an article which he personally found to be of seminal importance, he said, even if he would contest certain details. Then, not knowing what to do with his hands, he stood up and, pulling on his sleeves, proposed they have a drink at his place, adding almost timidly that he had put a bottle to chill and prepared some canapés. Almost immediately, as if he had gone too far, he hastened to add to Madame Pons-Romanov that it was really nothing, that he had simply put some Kerrling salmon roe caviar on a few biscuits and opened a jar of rollmops.

Kaltz who, in the corridor, continued to heap lavish praise on Madame Pons-Romanov's article, of which, without going into too much detail, he could not help but recognize the impact, stopped gallantly outside the door of Monsieur's apartment to allow Madame Pons-Romanov to go ahead and, his eyes lowered, lingered dreamily for a moment over the curve of her thighs and joined her on the landing to open his door. They went in, soon followed by Monsieur, his hands in his pockets, to whom Kaltz, turning round, said that he had done well to come along.

In the sitting room where Kaltz invited them, a huge cleaning job had apparently just been done, leaving only a plausible disorder, a spectacle case abandoned on a low table for example, a book left open on the arm of a chair. No sooner had they come in, moreover, than Kaltz hastened to excuse the mess and, closing the book, put it back in the bookshelf with such suavity that Monsieur suspected him of rehearsing the gesture. Madame Pons-Romanov, without the slightest eye for Kaltz's efforts, had immediately gone to stand by the window and, peering out, shivered and wrapped her arms around her fur coat. Monsieur, who realized after a moment that she was looking at him in the reflection of the glass, showed a somewhat embarrassed smile and, while Kaltz announced that he'd get the champagne, walked around the room and started to examine the book case where, between the books, samples of rock had been placed, the rarest of which were displayed behind glass in a separate cabinet. He bent down to read the names of a few rocks on the labels indicating their type and origin, then took a seat. Madame Pons-Romanov then slowly removed her fur coat which, without turning, she put down beside her on the back of a chair and, finally spinning round, walking slowly, measuring with her eyes the effect she produced, sat down in her soft woollen dress which clearly showed the scarcely disguised traces of her old-fashioned underwear.

Back in the room Kaltz, pushing a loaded tea trolley, crossed over nonchalantly and asked Madame Pons-Romanov when she thought she could start work on the maps then, modestly placing the ice bucket on the low table, sat down on the couch, the white towel for the champagne over his forearm. Madame Pons-Romanov said that at present she still had one or two jobs to finish, but that after that it was a promise; she wouldn't fail to dedicate herself to their work. Monsieur nodded his head, looking pensively at the walls, where there hung African masks, shields. You might open the champagne, Kaltz said to him. A rollmop? he added politely to Madame Pons-Romanov, advancing his hand towards the plate as an invitation to help herself.

Monsieur, taking his time getting up, took the towel from Kaltz's forearm and, unfolding it, took from the bucket a bottle, not of champagne but of sparkling wine which, pretending not to notice, he uncorked the way they do in Reims, turning the bottle anti-clockwise, the cork prudently pointed at Kaltz who kept an eye on him to watch what he was doing. Madame Pons-Romanov, who had already turned down a rollmop and who had just let them know that she didn't drink alcohol, careful all the same to do a minimum of honor to Kaltz's hospitality, said, seeking confirmation from Monsieur, that it seemed to her, but perhaps she was mistaken, in which case it really didn't matter, that Kaltz had mentioned biscuits with Kerrling. I would have forgotten all about them, said Kaltz and, getting up, he left to get them in the kitchen, asking her if, rather than champagne, she'd like a Schweppes instead.

When Kaltz returned from the kitchen, he sat down and poured the Schweppes into a champagne glass, watching the bubbles as if they were part of an experiment, and tried to explain to Madame Pons-Romanov the principal elements of his work. Admitting that he was uncomfortable about having extracts read too early, he asked her nonetheless, holding out her glass to her, if she would be interested to see the first pages and, as Madame Pons-Romanov, although far from seeming interested, put up no real fight but simply opened her hands with a fatalistic gesture of powerlessness and resignation, Kaltz asked Monsieur to fetch the manuscript.

Monsieur came back a little later with the manuscript, which he placed on the low table. Kaltz opened it and, putting on his glasses, told Monsieur, while leafing carelessly through the pages, that Madame Pons-Romanov had invited him to spend the coming weekend at her country place where she was having a few friends to stay, yes, adding that she had also proposed that Monsieur join them so as not to delay him in his work. You'll be sure to bring your typewriter, he said, taking off his glasses. A small typewriter of rather poor quality, he apologized to Madame Pons-Romanov, but very easy to carry.

The night of their arrival, at dusk, before the brightly-lit house from which the sounds of far-off voices reached them through the open french windows, Madame Pons-Romanov and Monsieur raked the dead leaves at the bottom of the garden. After stacking the tools in the shed and straightening out the rakes, they walked back to the house, where she introduced him to an elderly couple before they went upstairs, still talking quietly. She entered her room and, pushing Monsieur back with one finger, said, while closing the door with a voluptuous gesture, that she was going to change, no doubt slip on a skirt.

As Monsieur's room was on the second floor and the sound of numerous comings and goings could be heard from the stairs, Monsieur, not knowing what to do, decided to wait there and walked back and forth in the hallway, now and then approaching the stairwell to throw a quick glance over the rail. Finally, fearing he might be discovered unoccupied, he took a book from a small table and sat down in a chair, out of the way, beside a chest of drawers. Sitting there, the book on his knees, he opened it to give himself the right look should someone come along. It was Kaltz, finally, who appeared in the corridor dressed up in a splendid suit, his shirt immaculate and his bow-tie perfectly arranged. He found Monsieur deeply immersed in his book and proposed that, rather than stay there doing nothing, they go down together to join the other guests. Monsieur, interrupting his reading, put the book back in its place and asked Kaltz if, beforehand, they couldn't go to his room as he wanted to put on a tie, the one everybody envied, but Kaltz said that he was fine like that and, as they went downstairs, even went so far as to say that he shouldn't wear a tie at all, finding that he would not look good with his tie and his yellow sweater.

Madame Pons-Romanov's husband, who was apparently in the import-export business, was involved in a variety of concerns, stockmarket and financial, though no one could really say exactly what he did, nor could he himself, to judge by the way he was talking about them. Quite a few of the Romanovs' friends were there in the room, having drinks before the fireplace, the most prestigious of whom were a Secretary of State who until then had been wholly unknown to Monsieur, even right down to the existence of his portfolio, and an American scientist who hadn't yet arrived. When she made her entrance wearing a tight skirt, Madame Pons-Romanov, who had put her hair up in a severe bun, was introduced to the guests she didn't yet know: several women, men who stood up. The Secretary of State was an austere man, serenely dressed, his deep-black hair slicked back, who wore large horn glasses behind which floated an equivocal look that could break your career. He bowed to kiss Madame Pons-Romanov's hand and told her in a grief-stricken tone that he was very pleased to make her acquaintance. Having said this, he smiled in contained satisfaction and sat down in his armchair again, pulling on the creases of his trousers. Then, sitting up very straight, his head bent slightly forward, he followed the conversation sporting a benign look, rolling his maharajah eyes about him now and then.

While Monsieur, his eyes lowered, discreetly admired the quality of his leather shoes, which, crossing his legs, he had managed to show off under a lamp, Romanov, well entrenched in his armchair, a glass of whiskey in hand, explained to the Secretary of State who could hardly believe his ears that according to recent revelations by the journal *East-West,* whose impartiality could not be put in question, he said, unless you're a Communist of course, several new radar installations had been erected in Soviet territory at Olenegorsk, Pechora, Sary-Shagan, Lyaki and Pushkino. And at Krasnoyarsk, I believe, he added to be perfectly accurate, while Kaltz had found an elderly woman beside him with whom he could discuss his book.

In his room, after dinner, Monsieur didn't go to bed right away. No. He turned off the light and stood near the window, barefoot, looking at the garden for a while, at the symmetrical garden paths and the dark terraced lawns stretching off into the distance. Then, when all the lights were out and everything was black, he opened the window and, looking at the sky over the dark tips of the trees, tried in vain to imagine man-made satellites with their unbroken trails of light.

Yes, Monsieur displayed in all things a listless drive.

For lunch the next day the Romanovs made shish kebabs for their guests on an automatically heat-controlled barbecue at the end of the terrace. Each time a light flashed over one of the twelve spit compartments of the barbecue which, with smoke billowing from its burners, gave every impression of being on the brink of taking off at any moment, the slightly agitated Romanov, a napkin around his waist and a fork in his gloved hand, lifted the skewer from the grill, replaced it immediately with another, and rewound with a perplexed look the timer of the appropriate compartment. For this improvised shish kebab fare, Madame Pons-Romanov had judged it more convivial not to set a formal table. On the tawny table cloth, two large unfussy trays had been set out, one for the condiments, the mustards, pickles, peppers, the little pots of mayonnaise, of bearnaise, of hot and mild tomato and madeira sauces, and the other piled high with plates, a simple arrangement, just heavenly. Sitting at the bottom of the stairs, Kaltz had taken off his jacket and had opened his shirt. Leaning backwards, he was discussing Italian cinema with the Secretary of State. You know, it's been years since I went to the cinema, the Secretary of State was saying. Fellini, Kaltz went on all the same, Comencini, Antonioni, ah, Antonioni, he added, Antonioni. Really, I no longer have much time to see films, said the Secretary of State. Alas, nor do I, Kaltz admitted. They bemoaned their fate, became sad, toyed with the idea of giving up their jobs.

After lunch, Monsieur beat the Secretary of State at ping-pong twenty-one to four; then, sauntering round the table, trailing his bat behind him, he unenthusiastically proposed a rematch, but the Secretary of State, rather than be beaten once again by this unpleasant, probably Communist young man, chose to say no so he could read quietly in the sun. When Monsieur returned among the guests, coffee had been served in the garden; a few people came and went on the paths, some dozed in deck chairs. Seated not far from there, well, well, Madame Pons-Romanov was drinking her coffee in the company of Kaltz. I think it's time for a siesta, said Kaltz, and, getting up casually, he went off, discreetly following on Madame Pons-Romanov's heels.

The wife of the Secretary of State, a rather fat but elegant young woman, spent practically all afternoon on the terrace, sitting in a wicker chair, her knees tucked under her chin, plucking the hairs from her legs with a minuscule pair of tweezers. Now and then, lifting her head lazily, she peered from under her hair at whomever had the nerve to speak to her—and sighed. No, she didn't want anything to drink. No, she didn't want to go for a walk. What she wanted was to be left in peace: she had her hands full, and summer was on its way.

On this dreamy afternoon, Kaltz reclined on a patio swing-seat on his return from the siesta and, to unwind, read a book he had found in the house, closing the book from time to time to take a sip of orange juice and light a cigarette, smoked quietly and observed without a great deal of interest the quiet gardener who was pruning the rose bushes (without immediately noticing, moreover, that, under the straw hat, it was Monsieur), his only complaint Romanov's trap-shooting, which made him jump at regular intervals.

Having found momentary refuge among the roses, which he clipped with care before cutting suckers from each, Monsieur was soon joined by Hugo, the Romanovs' son, who, trying to befriend Monsieur, hadn't stopped pestering him since the beginning of the afternoon for a game of ping-pong. Unable to get rid of him, Monsieur ceded finally to the pressure of his mother who had joined in on her son's behalf, and granted him a game of ping-pong. I'll give you a five-point lead, sport, he said picking up the bat. You're joking, said Hugo. All right, nine points, said Monsieur graciously. Monsieur, the bigshot. You're joking, said Hugo, at ping-pong I'm tops. And in fact, the game was quite close. Monsieur had rolled up his sleeves and taken off his shoes. Barefoot, peeved, covered in sweat (you should really stop playing, exclaimed Madame Pons-Romanov, you're all flushed), he fought to hold his own. Hugo played with perfect skill, supple and agile, lifting, lifting, smashing—unstoppable. Furious, digging in his heels, Monsieur, another man, an ugly look on his face, pulled up his trouser legs and removed his watch to catch his breath. When, near the end of the game, he managed to contain some of his smashes to win several points in a row, Hugo conceded that he could have been quite good at ping-pong in his better days.

Proceeding from these few basic facts, it is now necessary to return to the symmetry of the crystal which, reflected at the level of the unit cell is a figure formed by the sum of the lines emerging from the same arbitrarily chosen points that are parallel to the crystallographic axes in relation to which any given property of the lattice will be identical, this holding true for all properties the symmetry of the lattice being the symmetry common to each one of the properties.

They worked little more than an hour at the end of the afternoon, Kaltz and Monsieur, calmly, hidden away in a small room on the second floor. Then Kaltz rearranged his papers and suggested they take a last walk before heading back to Paris. They walked side by side down to the bottom of the garden; Kaltz, relaxed, commented on the progress of his work while a pink light, far off, started to cover the house. Stopping at the fence that closed off the garden path which separated it from the trap-shooting range, they cut across the lawn to reach the house, where a few lights shone in the windows upstairs. Kaltz, his arms outstretched, breathed deeply and explained that it was his dream to be able to live in the country like this, surrounded by nature.

Back in Paris, they were dropped in front of their apartment by the Secretary of State who had stayed remarkably calm in the dense traffic, shifting gear, going back to neutral, while his wife beside him regretted not having commandeered motorcyclists to clear their way. Sitting in the back next to Monsieur, Kaltz, who didn't seem at all put off by the idea of coming back into Paris escorted by motorcyclists, suggested they stop and call at a pay phone. Yes, yes, he said, stop over there and, bending over the front seat, he started to insist. Monsieur, knowing that he always got his way in the end, wouldn't have liked to be in the shoes of the Secretary of State (who managed nonetheless to remain very polite making clear that it was entirely out of the question).

On their landing, turning to say goodnight, Monsieur thanked Kaltz for the weekend and, as he was about to take his key from his pocket, Kaltz invited him to have a bite to eat, adding that he had a surprise for him. Not another word, he said. He got him to enter his apartment and, directing him towards the kitchen, sat him down on a chair by pressing him lightly on his shoulders. Then, when he felt sure that Monsieur would stay put, he disappeared a brief instant and came back with the surprise, photocopies of drawings he had done in preparation for the maps, dozens of sketches and reliefs of compact cubic constructions which he took one by one from quite a handsome plastic container. Leaving Monsieur to admire the whole thing at his leisure, he brought from the refrigerator several plates and a silver platter, on which some rather shrivelled rollmops had started to go brown around their toothpicks. He then put out knives and forks, glasses and plates, and set a bottle of Beaujolais on the table. Unfortunately I don't have a corkscrew, he said, but it doesn't matter, does it, we can drink water. Monsieur, complying, put the drawings back in the folder and, getting up, said he'd get a corkscrew from his flat.

Monsieur returned quite a bit later—he couldn't have known, no, he couldn't have known that he should never have gone home that evening—with the corkscrew, which he put on the table. Kaltz asked him what was wrong. Nothing, said Monsieur, I got a call from my brother. He sat down in silence. Examining the corkscrew discreetly, Kaltz, in a low voice, asked if it was something serious. No, no, said Monsieur, not really, he's going to the opera tonight and he asked me to baby-sit his daughters.

When he showed up at his brother's, Monsieur had to ring repeatedly before someone opened the door. Through the crack, a young woman who was getting ready to go out asked him what he wanted. Monsieur, with a knowing smile, slipped past her and went in, and proceeded calmly to his nieces' room. In the entrance hall, he was stopped by another young woman who, alerted by the first, barred his way to ask, again, what he wanted. At this point, Monsieur's brother appeared (oh, hello, he said) in a dinner jacket and, having asked him how he was, introduced him to the young women, Anne and Benedicte, both teachers of philosophy. Monsieur kissed them on their cheeks and, standing with them in the hall, all sparkles, asked his brother around what time he thought he'd be back.

Monsieur's brother (also a philosopy teacher, but it was not for Monsieur to judge his brother's conduct) had two little girls, Monsieur's nieces, twins of six and six. Monsieur, who had patiently and carefully examined them from time to time, could now tell them apart at first glance. You, you're Jeanne, he said, pointing his finger, and you, Clotilde. Yes, that's right, they squealed, overjoyed. One of them, Clotilde, was very lively, wild and full of fun, and the other rather amorphous, like her uncle.

To arouse their interests which were so tender at that age, Monsieur had resolved, each time he came to look after them, to put the time to good use and teach them to play chess. He put a chess board on a low table in the middle of the room, and sat cross-legged on the carpet. The twins, facing him, were spellbound. While he explained the movements of the pieces, standing side by side in their undershirts and cotton panties, they listened attentively, tiny and completely absorbed. Don't pick your nose, said Monsieur, while I'm talking.

The lessons progressed, the girls started to know how to move the pieces. When they were thinking hard, Monsieur found them adorable, absolutely his nieces. He particularly liked their way of saying "J'ajuste" when, as he had taught them, they touched a piece they hadn't planned to move. In fact this was the only thing they really liked about chess, being able to say "J'ajuste," and Monsieur finally suspected them of touching pieces just for the fun of saying "J'ajuste."

When, that evening, Monsieur came into his nieces' bedroom, they were playing with a hair dryer, fighting over the appliance, then shooting air underneath the posters that decorated the walls. Monsieur sat on the bed without speaking, which was enough for them to become vaguely frightened of him and, unsure of themselves, they tired of their game. Monsieur unplugged the hair dryer and told them it was time to go to bed. Then, wheeling round, he did a half-hearted imitation of a crash-landing glider, which had always made them laugh. We do understand each other, eh? he said. He sat down beside them and, tucking them in, kissed them on their four cheeks. We do understand each other, eh? he repeated wistfully. What did you say, Uncle? On second thoughts, they didn't understand a thing.

Native gold, found in nature in the state of simple bodies, is often finely disseminated in the quartz gangue of auriferous lodes, and in sulphides, pyrite for example, mispickel, two i's, pyrrhotite, two r's followed by an h, and stibnite, as it's pronounced.

Monsieur, anxious all the same to get out from time to time, took his nieces to the Palais de la Découverte one Saturday afternoon. They flew through the rooms, the girls trotting quite far behind him, and, stopping now and then before an exhibit, Monsieur, never missing a chance to instruct them, tried to get them to understand life's basic principles, which were even more of a mystery for them than for him. After the visit, as they moved off down the street, Monsieur went on to explain that when they walked to the east, their speed was added to the speed of the earth's rotation, whereas when they moved to the west, it was subtracted. Buy us a pizza, Uncle, they said. A pizza, cried Monsieur stopping short and, looking around him for a passer-by to witness the outrage, he told them that at their age, you don't eat pizza. That's it. Now, he said, listen to me. In your opinion, if you want to escape from yourself, which I don't suggest you do, by the way, he continued, stopping on the sidewalk with hands in his pockets while the twins in pink anoraks, beneath him, lifted their heads to listen, is it better to walk to the east, or to the west? They didn't know. To the east, said Monsieur, grinning at them and wagging his finger, to the east, because time goes quicker that way. Every bit counts, he said, and started walking again. A pizza? At their age, a pizza?

In the evening, when he had no pages to copy, Monsieur, lying on his bed, peeled oranges decoratively, working them with a Swiss-Army knife to make aquatic plants, nenuphars or other water lilies. Aside from rare fleeting thoughts which, unformulated, vanished immediately in his head, Monsieur, in as much as he consented to go on, no longer had any notion of the flow of time, neither to the east, nor to the west. Previously, he could easily have imagined two distinct entities, unhappily abstract, separate at all points, of which one, immobile, was himself who had always been rather sedentary, and the other was time, moving over his body, whereas at present the idea was coming to light inside him that there were not two entities, but only one, a vast movement that bore him irresistibly away.

The interpretation of Greek terms employed to identify the exterior forms of crystals—yoohoo, are you listening—is in point of fact easy, if not immediate, and presents no difficulty, even for the layman; pinacoid, for example, from pinax, plank, signifying two parallel planes while pentagonohexaoctahedron, from hexa and octo, means a solid of six times eight equals forty-eight pentagonal planes.

The following evening, peace to those of good will, Monsieur moved into the Leguens' apartment.

When he arrived, Monsieur Leguen, who was waiting for him in the hall, wanted to introduce him immediately to his wife and son. Yes, yes, said Monsieur and, as the taxi was waiting below, first things first, he asked if someone could help him with his things. Ludovic didn't seem too thrilled by the idea, but followed Monsieur grudgingly down the stairs, casual and distant, helped the driver unload the taxi and carried up the suitcases in two trips, taking them to Monsieur's room.

In his room, Monsieur removed the lace bedspread, folded it in two and lay down on the blankets. He untied his tie. Without getting up, he took off his shoes one after the other, letting them fall to the floor. He remained still a few moments, relieved at not having a neighbour any longer, opened his hands, stopped breathing, or near enough.

There's a test in physics tomorrow, said Ludovic, coming into his room. He put his physics textbook on the edge of the bed and, without another word, went to the window and looked out, despondent. Monsieur sat up in bed after a moment and, lighting a cigarette (in his view, he was too calm), asked what the test was on, and what he had to prepare for. The relativity of movement, he said. Monsieur dragged on his cigarette and, opening the book, asked if that was the lesson to be reviewed. Obviously, he said, the relativity of movement, there's no exercise.

Obviously, said Monsieur. Having flipped rapidly through the textbook, he came to the right page and started to read. Movement, he read, its relative character. That's the title, he said; you understand what it means, at least? Of course he understood, they'd done it yesterday in class, movement its relative character. Good. When a point is mobile in a field, it does not suffice to know its coordinates, one must equally know when it occupies those coordinates. Time then intervenes in two ways in the domain of physics, in its duration on the one hand, the interval of time elapsed between the beginning and the end of the observed phenomenon; in its date on the other, the instant at which the event takes place. Repeat, he said. Now? asked Ludovic, who continued to look out of the window. In your own words, said Monsieur. And, while still looking out of the window, Ludovic repeated that the duration was the interval of time that elapsed between the beginning and the end and that the date, that was the moment when this happened, Monsieur, without making a sound, went out of the room and left the apartment on tiptoe. Downstairs, in the street, he posted himself on the pavement opposite and saw Ludovic behind the window, coming to the end of reciting his lesson (people, really).

Monsieur, arms folded, didn't move and nearly smiled, immobile in the street. Perhaps seeing Monsieur there, before him on the pavement when he should have been behind him in the room, Ludovic, in a fit of giddiness, would imagine that Monsieur, who obviously could be in only one place at one time, displaced himself apparently without transition and that his energy, like that of the electron, in its sleight of hand (hip, hop), effected a discontinuous leap at a certain moment, but that it was impossible to determine at which moment this leap would take place as there was no reason, according to the Copenhagen interpretation, for it to happen at one given moment rather than at another. But, in Monsieur's opinion, he wouldn't understand. No (it wasn't part of the lesson).

Monsieur then walked around, ambled slowly through the streets. He looked in the windows of record shops, clothing shops—bought some shoes. Indeed. Coming out of the shoe shop, ever more thoughtful, he bought a newspaper in the square and entered a café, his shoebox in his hands.

The café was nearly empty, and Monsieur sat down in an alcove on a rather faded bench, brown and cracked in spots. He took the shoes from their box, freeing them from their many layers of tissue paper and, slipping his hand into one, considered it for a few moments in profile. Then, putting them back, he placed the box next to him and ordered a beer, then unfolded his paper. At a nearby table, by the pay phone, two men were looking rather forelorn. Monsieur quickly suspected that the younger one, who, since he'd come in, had not stopped glancing furtively about, visibly agitated, would not hesitate to ask him something, an enquiry or request, maybe even touch him for money. And sure enough, finally addressing Monsieur, he asked if he didn't have something to write with. Thinking it over, Monsieur closed his paper and said no. I do have my fountain pen, he said, but I never lend it, it's one of my rules (Monsieur had few rules, but he held to them). Then, as the young man seemed disappointed, Monsieur, coming around, took his pen from his inside pocket and said that if he handed him his paper, he didn't mind writing for him. Oh, by all means, said the young man and, getting up to take a seat beside him, he invited the older man to sit opposite them at Monsieur's table. This might take some time, he said.

Well, explained the young man, I'm a history student and I'm writing my dissertation on the Lycée at Chartres during the phoney war. Why the Lycée at Chartres, you will ask? he said and, without waiting for an answer, he acknowledged straight away that it was a perfectly arbitrary choice, but that he had hoped to focus on a concrete event, so that he could refer to the local archives by going into the field himself, and so that also, to the extent that it was possible, he could try to meet eyewitnesses who had lived through the period. Furthermore, said the young man, Chartres being in the Eure-et-Loir, the Administrator of that region in 1939 was Jean Moulin, which is rather interesting, don't you think? So, he said, for my paper, I first put together a list of all the students who attended the Lycée Marceau in 1939; I wrote informing them of my project and asking if they would agree to collaborate with me giving me their account, and Monsieur Levasseur, he said, indicating the other man who, seeing himself introduced, bowed his head modestly, has agreed to tell us of his school year during 1939–1940. And you don't have a pen either? asked Monsieur. No, said Monsieur Levasseur opening his hands, sorry.

Right, said the young man, we'll start. I'd like to ask you, Monsieur Levasseur, first question, what were the major upsets particular to the year 1939, at the beginning of the school year, for example. Well, said Monsieur Levasseur, sitting up in his chair and putting his hands together, personally I was awarded the first part of my leaving diploma in June, but I believe I remember that the oral examinations that year weren't held in Paris but at Chartres, inside the Lycée itself, which brought on the upsets you may well imagine. At the time, what was your state of mind? asked Monsieur, tapping the table.

My state of mind? said Monsieur Levasseur, glancing discreetly at the young man to see if he should also respond to Monsieur's questions; well, he said, the young man having given him the go-ahead with a tacit blink, we thought that, sooner or later, we'd be mobilized. We hadn't forgotten, you see, that in 1914 even the youngest classes had been called up and we thought that it was going to be the same for us. So the whole year there was a feeling of things being more or less provisional which was brutally resolved on the tenth of May 1940 with the German offensive. That day, I remember very well, I went to the railway station with a Czech friend who was leaving for the front. After Hitler's occupation of Czechoslovakia, a lot of Czech soldiers had left their country and some, who had been in the air force, wound up at the Chartres air field (can you speak just a little bit slower? asked Monsieur).

Could you tell us, Monsieur Levasseur, the young man said when Monsieur had taken this down, what changed after the tenth of May 1940? Well, said Monsieur Levasseur taking a quick sip of his drink, for the younger classes there was practically no change, everything went on as if nothing had happened. But for us, on the other hand, we tried to make ourselves useful, working for the Red Cross for example, or for the shelter for refugees. Good, said Monsieur, thank you. And right up until the thirteenth of June, Monsieur Levasseur went on, the date when everyone left Chartres. Yes, yes, said Monsieur soothingly, and he got up to leave.

Back at the Leguens', using the key he'd been given, Monsieur ventured into the corridor and crossed the dining room, where the same old woman was still eating, good evening Madame, and walked through the apartment to get to his room. There, lying on the bed with his arms folded over his chest, breathing slowly, Monsieur became suddenly aware that he was too calm. He knew well enough that he should try to be more annoyed by the circumstances of life, little by little, in steps, to avoid the tensions he was storing up exploding all of a sudden with one big bang.

Very softly, someone knocked on the door. Very softly. Visibly embarrassed to be bothering Monsieur, the old woman coming in explained to him that she had mislaid a shawl and that she hardly dared to come and see if, by any chance, she hadn't left it in her room. I'm Lucien's mother, she said, and she batted her eyelids, seemingly flattered. Then, as the conversation lagged, she searched the chest of drawers for her shawl and Monsieur looked on leaning on his elbow, and she told him in passing that it had been very painful for her to have to leave her room, very painful she said, but she added quickly that it wasn't Monsieur's fault, of course, it was her son who had talked her into it. You're a teacher, aren't you? she said gently.

In the domain of physics, when indicating the date, it is necessary to establish a temporal origin and to give it conventionally the date zero.

You listening? said Monsieur. Yes, yes, said Ludovic. To establish a chronology, an instrument is needed for measuring time. A clock for example, he said. A clock? said Ludovic, who seemed doubtful. Yes, said Monsieur in a pale voice, a clock. An electronic chronometer, more likely, said Ludovic. Go get your father please, said Monsieur (Monsieur was not particularly fond, no he was not, of being contradicted).

Monsieur explained to Monsieur Leguen that he had thought it over and that the room, in fact, didn't suit him. He was terribly sorry. Maybe another time. He took out his cheque book and, cutting short any further discussion, uncapped his *Rotring* to pay a month's rent. Then, calling a taxi, he got Ludovic to take down his suitcases, wished him good luck in life in general and on his test in particular.

Back at his apartment, as Monsieur was getting ready to open his door, Kaltz appeared and, seeing Monsieur in the stairwell, said that his timing was perfect, he was just coming over. He had, in fact, written a short introductory note to his book, really nothing at all, he said, but he would be glad to share it with him, and before Monsieur had the time to say a word he switched on the hall light and started to read. He read out, our ambition is in no way an attempt to give in this short treatise an exhaustive view of the question we propose to discuss. Our ambition, rather, will be to present to the reader a sort of itinerary which, following our own tastes, will guide—and we hope, instruct—him, in a manner on which we insist: purely subjective. Very good, very good, said Monsieur, and he went in, leaving Kaltz on the stairs.

For several days afterwards, Monsieur did his best to avoid Kaltz.

Some mornings, after breakfast, when the weather was nice and he wasn't working, he left his apartment and went up to the top floor to go for walks. The roofs were perfect, in Monsieur's view, almost flat, joined by metal walkways. His walk over, Monsieur returned to his apartment and closed the door behind him without making a sound so as not to attract Kaltz's attention.

During his walks, confined, it's true, to a very limited perimeter, the only person Monsieur came across, apart from, one day, a neighbour who was installing a parabolic antenna and stopped what he was doing for a moment to watch him go by, was a slightly greying man of fifty or so, dressed in an old-fashioned green velvet suit, who wandered around slowly with a plastic bag in his hand, seemingly weighing up the pros and cons. Monsieur usually gave him a wide berth, because he was wary, to tell the truth, of this type of character.

For a change Monsieur sometimes took a chair with him onto the roof. On the fifth floor he climbed outside, then, crouching beside the trap door, pulled the chair behind him and went to sit down a little off to one side, on a platform that ran along the façade. He found a place in the shelter of the awning and sat there, perfectly calm.

Monsieur, now more than ever, always sat on a chair. He asked for no more from life, Monsieur, than a chair. There, hovering between two compromises, he sought refuge in the calming performance of simple gestures. When at work for example (the job was a breeze), he would peel an orange at his desk, his wrinkled handkerchief flat on the table, to the admiration of the secretaries. No one on the sixteenth floor could complain about Monsieur. Madame Dubois-Lacour found him a remarkable young man, this Monsieur, knowledgeable, calm, serious, punctual.

At the office, when things weren't busy, Monsieur went downstairs to the cafeteria and read the paper. Across from him in the glass entrance hall, here and there, small flower pots boasted benjamina or papyrus, and two or three receptionists, quite another matter, talked on the telephone behind the circular counter. Often, before going back up to his office, Monsieur, going round the counter, good afternoon ladies, stood for a while in front of the aquarium and watched the fish with his hands in his pockets, never tiring of contemplating the inaccessible purity of the trajectories they traced with such languor.

Monsieur now managed, but only felt a fleeting pride each time he succeeded in so doing, to get up to his office without taking his hands out of his pockets. He would wait as long as necessary in front of the aquarium, his hands in his pockets, for someone to arrive and call the elevator. Then, when the automatic doors opened beside him, he got in first and placed himself at the back, in the right corner, as far as possible from the buttons. There, adopting a low profile, he would wait for someone to ask him which floor he was going to and, nothing easier, told them.

In his office, Monsieur worked at keeping his eyes down, and even closed them sometimes, *fiat lux,* when he was alone. If, in the course of a discussion, a divergence of views happened to arise, he tried not to rock the boat, Monsieur, contenting himself in the thought that he alone was in a position to fully savour his silence. His interlocutors, what's more, quite liked him; and some, without going so far as applauding or flattering him, even found him affable, because of a certain way he had of smiling economically so as not to tarnish his image as a man of discourse.

In his office, a large number of objects were neatly ordered on Monsieur's desk, letter opener, pencil sharpener, pocket calculator.

Air conditioning, too.

Sometimes, bursting into his office, Dubois-Lacour asked Monsieur if he couldn't meet some sales representatives in her place as she had to leave and doubted if she'd have the time, she said, to brief them herself. Monsieur said yes, if that would help, and asked if he should brief them together or separately. Choosing generally to meet them all together, Monsieur gathered his thoughts by pacing his office with his hands clasped under his chin before confronting them. Then, opening the door, he quickly went and sat down while ten or so people came in jostling into position and placing themselves in an arc around his desk to hear him speak. Good, good, any other questions, gentlemen, said Monsieur before closing. No. And Madame? he added inclining his head respectfully toward the only woman present, not bad either, at least from a distance. People, really.

One night, after dinner, Monsieur went up onto the roof—and left it all quietly behind, his chair in his hand.

It was night now, Monsieur could hardly be mistaken. Night had fallen over Paris. So had rain, apparently, a little earlier; the roofs were grey, shiny, a little slippery. In the distance windows were lit up, the streets seemed deserted below. Placing his chair at the edge of the roof, he took his lighter from his pocket and, lifting his head and lighting a cigarette, casually considered the sky, pure and clear after the rain, around Orion. Standing beside the chair, Monsieur remained for a long time looking at the sky and, as he deepened his vision, distinguishing now a network of stellar points and lines, the sky became in his mind a gigantic metro map illuminating the night. He sat down and, starting from Sirius which he located easily, he moved towards Montparnasse-Bienvenue, went as far as Sèvres-Babylone and, taking his time at Betelgeux, arrived at Odéon, which was his final destination.

There, in his mind, the same night lights twinkled on.

Monsieur knew almost nothing of Anna Bruckhardt, really. He had met her only once, at a party given by the Dubois-Lacours. At the end of the evening, they'd spoken together for two hours, hardly more, sitting opposite each other in the kitchen among the empty glasses, eating from time to time, she a narrow slice of chocolate cake that she cut meticulously with a knife, and Monsieur a large spoonful of mixed salad, first taking out the nuts, which he'd personally always found disgusting. Now and then, Dubois-Lacour made a quick appearance in the kitchen to get a bottle of champagne from the refrigerator. They hardly noticed her, Anna Bruckhardt and Monsieur, and continued to talk quietly about this and that, but without asking questions, out of discretion, so that all evening they hadn't exchanged the slightest bit of information concerning themselves. No, they told each other anecdotes instead, taking turns, which, as they went on, became more and more insignificant, about people that the other didn't know and that they themselves hardly knew anyway. Now and then one guest or another, glass in hand, came into the kitchen to see what was happening and, as nothing was happening there, after idling a while beside the table, left as they had come, glass in hand. In this way, far from the noises of merrymaking and the Brazilian rhythms, Anna Bruckhardt and Monsieur now became accomplices exchanging looks, nothing escaped Monsieur's lowered eyes, nor did they tire of telling each other stories, leaning on their elbows, finding out about unimportant and complicated facts that didn't concern them. Anna Bruckhardt was now in the middle of telling Monsieur a particularly unedifying anecdote which had them in stitches when they were joined in the kitchen by a group of guests who, without a word, took away the chairs around the table and sat a little distance away, beside the window, taking with them a pile of plates and a bowl of fruit salad. There, between bites, they started telling each other about their vacations in Egypt, regretting quickly enough not being able to show their slides along with the descriptions they gave of the grandiose, often totally unreal countryside (people, really). Anna Bruckhardt and Monsieur, after a while, finally decided to get up and leave the kitchen. They lingered a moment in the hall, exchanged one final story in the dark, and then fell silent, perfectly silent, immobile, looking at each other with melancholy eyes, Monsieur with his back to the wall, she facing him, a hand on his shoulder.

That was all.

Around Monsieur, now, it was like night itself. Immobile on his chair, his head bent back, he once again let his view mingle with the infinity of the skies, his mind reaching out towards the curve of the horizon. Breathing peacefully, he scanned the whole night of thought, all of it, far into the memory of the universe, to the depths of the glimmering sky. Reaching ataraxy, no thoughts stirred in Monsieur's mind, but his mind was the world—that he'd convened.

Yes. He was beginning to be embarrassed, Monsieur.

After a while, perhaps starting to get a bit cold which struck him as somewhat extravagant, he resolved to get up and, raising the collar of his jacket, went back the way he'd come, thoughtfully pulling his chair after him through the night. Coming to the trap door, he opened it and, kneeling awkwardly on the roof, how else could it be done, slowly lowered the chair to the ground. When it was firmly on the floor, pivoting while holding onto the sill with both hands, Monsieur let himself gently down to the chair. Then, closing the trap door, he dusted off his sleeves, fixed his tie.

When Monsieur accompanied Anna Bruckhardt to a taxi stand after the Dubois-Lacours' party, walking beside her in the deserted streets, he wondered if he couldn't, in the course of the conversation, take a hand from his pocket to look at his palm in an offhand way and, prolonging the movement, casually take her arm to help her cross the street. They walked side by side, Monsieur looking surreptitiously around him in search of a street crossing. He didn't find one, and Anna Bruckhardt, getting up on tiptoe, finally hailed a taxi with a simplicity of gesture he had to admire.

Then Monsieur went to his room and called Anna Bruckhardt to say that he wanted to have dinner with her.

That evening.

Night lights had shone on the Place de l'Odéon. From his first meeting with Anna Bruckhardt, a month earlier, Monsieur remembered that instant with painful precision, night lights on the Place de l'Odéon. At regular intervals the traffic lights switched color, changing his perspective. On the other side, shutters covered the storefronts, the cinemas were closed. Monsieur stood in the centre of the square; a man walked down a side street, a couple went over a pedestrian crossing. It was two in the morning, maybe three—and Monsieur had left Anna Bruckhardt in a taxi a few seconds earlier.

Anna Bruckhardt couldn't free herself that evening, but they had dinner the next day. They had arranged to meet in the bar of a big hotel.

Monsieur had arrived early and, sitting in a low armchair, looked at the people around him, of whom there were few, and whose faces took on pale hues under the dim lights of the room. It was a comfortable place. Elderly men sipped their drinks, chewed on olives, peanuts. Some read the paper; others, accompanied by women, remained silent, sitting comfortably. One of them looked peacefully about him from time to time and took a small sip of his drink. A record turned slowly on the stereo behind the bar, emitting a muted concerto for flute and harp.

Not having found a taxi, Monsieur had come to their rendezvous by metro. A young man had got into his carriage at Franklin-Roosevelt station and immediately asked him, rather nervously, if the seat next to his was free; Monsieur looked at the seat, which was in fact free, it would have been difficult to deny it. The young man sat down beside him, lifted the collar of his bomber jacket. Monsieur moved over a bit. The metro thundered into the tunnel, and they travelled side by side, Monsieur looking out of the window, and he at the floor, at Monsieur's new shoes. At the next station, the young man quickly got out, leaving his suitcase, which a passenger immediately, all but jostling Monsieur, hastened to throw onto the platform. Very curious, indeed, said Anna Bruckhardt, and she took off her coat, not having had the time to do so beforehand for, as soon as she'd arrived, Monsieur had started into his anecdote.

Monsieur, a fund of anecdotes.

The bar of the hotel had livened up around them now. The waiter, who had hitherto ignored them, came and asked them what they'd have, and they ordered two bourbons. They remained silent while waiting for the drinks, both somewhat embarrassed, exchanging a glance now and then. The waiter finally brought their bourbons and put a dish of peanuts on the table. Leaning forward occasionally to take a peanut, Anna Bruckhardt and Monsieur, still silent, looked at the decoration on the walls, examined the list of drinks. Monsieur could certainly have reanimated the conversation and he had thought of doing so by throwing himself into another anecdote.

In the taxi on the way to the restaurant, after quite a long period of silence, when, sitting side by side on the back seat, they looked outside through their respective windows, they started talking vaguely about painting, literature. It's one of the few things he, Monsieur, would still have liked to do, paint, being the father of a school child, leading the quiet life, attending a parent-teacher meeting every few months, or write, even though he confided in her that he preferred light to words (yes, this was perhaps his open side, for once opting for life). And then, as Anna Bruckhardt remarked in this connection—apropos of what Monsieur didn't quite know, but that wasn't of much importance—the one didn't preclude the other. True, he said. Then, as the taxi was taking its time in all the traffic, they started to exchange more personal information, a little at random, here and there. And, for example, they learned that they were twenty-nine and thirty-four years old, while the driver, for his part, was forty-seven.

It was Anna Bruckhardt who had chosen the restaurant, and when, pushing open the glass door, she turned to say it was her favourite place, Monsieur took it as a sign that he had already acquired a certain special place in Anna Bruckhardt's heart. Before following her into the dining room, he made sure he had cigarettes and, while the head waiter invited Anna Bruckhardt to be seated, Monsieur, joining her with one hand in his pocket, perfectly at ease, sat down beside her. He then saw, looking up at the head waiter, that he was supposed to sit opposite. He got up discreetly and, pulling on the creases of his trousers, circled the table to sit down across from Anna Bruckhardt, who watched him with a somewhat worried look. After a minute they were presented with menus. Monsieur, a little ill-at-ease, turned his head each time the door opened behind him and, rotating slightly in his seat, took a look at the newcomers. Pom, pom. He closed the menu and, leaning across the table, told Anna Bruckhardt in a low voice that he had seen that they had salmon and, not to hide anything from her, he had nothing against one in a sorrel sauce. More anecdotes? she said, and smiling, she opted for the sea bass and fennel.

Monsieur, his head down, ate his fish in silence, occasionally looking outside at the small square lit up here and there by street lamps. Their table, in a covered terrace walled with glass panes, looked onto the columns of the Petit Odéon theater. It was a calm, even pleasant restaurant, which Monsieur could reproach for only one thing, precisely that it faced the street, as the passers-by sometimes stopped behind the glass to watch him eat. Anna Bruckhardt, far more discreet, didn't make such a thing of his presence; she ate gracefully across from him, taking her time to separate with a slow movement the fillets of her fish. She was beautiful like that, dressed in a white blouse and a suede jacket. At the top of her forehead she had a tiny pimple, adorable, which must surely have given her cause for embarrassment when she was getting ready to go out that evening.

There weren't many people in the restaurant, five tables at most were occupied around them. At the next table, a young woman was listening to her lover, a doctor in all likelihood, or perhaps he was her husband, who was going on about the question of surrogate motherhood, an important question, he was saying, to which two types of reactions are encountered. What right, in effect, say some, he said, putting down his knife and fork, has society to oppose the will of a couple who seriously want to have a child if this couple judges that the means proposed is appropriate and if the surrogate mother freely consents? He picked up his utensils and took a bite, thoughtful, when all of the lights in the restaurant suddenly went out.

Well. Monsieur raised his head, tried to distinguish Anna Bruckhardt across from him in the semi-darkness. In the room everyone had stopped eating, some were looking around. The doctor was the only one to risk a restrained applause, sitting upright in his chair, then continuing right on with his surrogate mothers, picked up his argument while lowering his voice all the same, as if it was necessary to whisper now that it was dark. And in fact, it was very dark. Not only was the whole room plunged in darkness, but outside there was no longer a single light. Nothing but a few buildings on the square with more pronounced shadows could be made out in the blackness. In the street, no more passers-by could be seen, all the street lights had gone out. Almost immediately the head waiter who, moreover, seemed not to have noticed, so much had his attitude remained the same, calm and poised, came to announce that candles were being prepared. Then, as if that wasn't enough, after a short while, he returned to announce that Monsieur Lacoste was wanted on the telephone. A shadow at the back of the room got up hesitantly amid the tables and, guiding himself in the dark with his lighter, went off into the depths of the restaurant.

Monsieur, his face pasted against the glass, tried to make out something in the street. But everything stayed black, the buildings remained dark, cut from a single block in the night. At the corner of the street, several pedestrians had lit lighters and others came forward to join their group. A car went by now and then, the lights tracing long oblique lines along the ground. Then all became dark again. Would you like a dessert, all the same? he said, or should I ask for the bill. When the bill came, Monsieur asked Anna Bruckhardt if she would like him to treat her or if she would rather pay half. Anna Bruckhardt had no preference. After a few moments of reflection, Monsieur admitted to her that he had no idea what was to be done in such cases. Anna Bruckhardt, reassuring him, said there was no fixed rule in the matter.

Perfect. In that case, it was perfectly insoluble. Then what do we do? said Monsieur and, lowering his head, he plunged himself into the contemplation of his fingers in the darkness.

Anna Bruckhardt, starting to smile at his perplexity, repeated that it was really as he pleased. Finally, coming to a compromise, Monsieur, seeing no other solution, suggested splitting the bill in four and paying three quarters himself (it was the simplest, he said, and of a certain mathematical elegance at the very least).

When, coming out of the restaurant, they began to make their way towards the Luxembourg gardens, they saw that the blackout extended apparently through the whole neighborhood, and perhaps beyond, who could tell. The streets, so calm as they walked by, were darker than they had ever seen them; now there was nothing to spoil the night. In front of the senate buildings the bars of the fence of the Luxembourg Gardens looked like a dark black portcullis. It had been more than twenty minutes now that the electricity had gone out, and, walking side by side, Anna Bruckhardt and Monsieur exchanged a few considerations on the consequences of the power failure and expressed a friendly thought for the people stuck in elevators (people, really). Becoming slightly outdistanced by Anna Bruckhardt, Monsieur found himself several paces behind her and, his hands in his pockets, walked with his head up, looking at the sky.

The sky in its natural state now, far from the parasitic city lights.

At Saint-Sulpice Square they sat down on a bench and stayed there for a long moment one next to the other, in perfect silence. The mind's eye, said Monsieur after a while, the mind's eye. I'm sorry, said Anna Bruckhardt, a bit surprised at his sudden loquacity. No, nothing, said Monsieur. Yes, something, said Anna Bruckhardt. Sight, said Monsieur. The mind's eye, yes. In the opinion of science at least, he added for the sake of honesty, and included with a vague hand motion the Copenhagen interpretation, the Tutti Quanta theory and all that. According to Prigogine, in fact, quantum theory destroys the notion that physical description can be accurate and that its language can represent the properties of a system independently of observational conditions. Well, well. Beside him on the bench, in perfect evidence, was Anna Bruckhardt's hand.

Discreetly watching Anna Bruckhardt's hand, Monsieur, his eyes lowered, eventually lifted one of her fingers, prudently, then a second, and finally he took her hand in his.

He stayed like that for a few moments, Monsieur, holding Anna Bruckhardt's hand, then, not knowing what to do with it, he delicately put it back down on the bench. Well, shall we go, he said. They got up and walked. In the apartments on the Boulevard Saint-Germain, here and there, shadows moved behind lace curtains. People were leaning out of windows, candles behind them, looking out onto the street. They walked on almost without speaking, Anna Bruckhardt and Monsieur, on they walked.

It was night itself on the Place de l'Odéon. Stopping in the square, Monsieur, his head raised, pointed his arm skyward and slowly traced with his finger the line Sirius-Aldebaran while explaining to Anna Bruckhardt that the Place de l'Odéon in his mind was that star there, Aldebaran. Which? said Anna Bruckhardt. There, said Monsieur, under the upturned A, the star that's almost orange. No, I can't see, said Anna Bruckhardt, who wasn't really listening, in fact, still peering at the sky beside him. Never mind, said Monsieur, we're there, and taking his lighter from his pocket, he lit it between their two faces. They looked at each other with melancholy eyes. Anna Bruckhardt touched his cheek, and kissed him, softly, in the night. Hip, hop. And presto, it was no more difficult than that.

Life, mere child's play, for Monsieur.

SELECTED DALKEY ARCHIVE PAPERBACKS

FOR A FULL LIST OF PUBLICATIONS, VISIT:
www.dalkeyarchive.com

SELECTED DALKEY ARCHIVE PAPERBACKS